THE NIGHTMARE CLUB

A DOG'S BREAKFAST

ANNIE GRAVES

ILLUSTRATED BY
GLENN McELHINNEY

MINNEAPOLIS

First published in Dublin, Ireland by Little Island
Original edition © Little Island 2011

American edition © 2015 Darby Creek,
a division of Lerner Publishing Group, Inc.

Main body text set in ITC Stone Serif Std.
Typeface provided by Adobe Systems.

Darby Creek
A division of Lerner Publishing Group, Inc.
241 First Avenue North
Minneapolis, MN 55401 USA

For reading levels and more information, look up this title
at www.lernerbooks.com.

Library of Congress Cataloging-in-Publication Data

Graves, Annie.
    A dog's breakfast / by Annie Graves ; illustrated by
Glenn McElhinney.
        pages   cm. — (The Nightmare Club)
    Originally published: Dublin, Ireland : Little Island,
2011.
    ISBN 978–1–4677–4350–1 (lib. bdg. : alk. paper)
    ISBN 978–1–4677–7634–9 (eBook)
    [1. Behavior—Fiction. 2. Transformation—Fiction.
3. Magic—Fiction. 4. Horror stories.] I. McElhinney,
Glenn illustrator. II. Title.
PZ7.G77512Dog 2015
[Fic]—dc23   2014015300

Manufactured in the United States of America
1 – SB – 12/31/14

For Hugh Shalby Nameless,
a kitten with attitude

Annie Graves is twelve years old, and she has no intention of ever growing up. She is, conveniently, an orphan, and lives at an undisclosed address in the Glasnevin area of Dublin, Ireland, with her pet toad, Much Misunderstood, and a small black kitten, Hugh Shalby Nameless. You needn't think she goes to school—pah!—or has anything as dull as brothers and sisters or hobbies, but let's just say she keeps a large cauldron on the stove.

This is not her first book. She has written eight, so far, none of which is her first.

Publisher's note: We did try to take a picture of Annie, but her face just kept fading away. We have sent our camera for investigation but suspect the worst.

THANK you!

I have to give a big thanks to Katherine Farmar, because if I don't, she'll send a fire-breathing demonic alien after me!

Annie here, from Glasnevin. I'm the author. That's a posh word for writer, in case you don't know. I'm not posh, but I do like posh words.

As well as being the author, I am the hostess. Which means it's my house where we have the Halloween sleepover every year. A gang of us all get together, girls in the big four-poster bed, boys in sleeping bags on the floor, and we scare each other to BITS. No costumes, no flashlights, no special effects.

Just really scary stories.

I have this great scary story. Being an author and all, I'm good at stories. For years now, I've been trying to tell it. It's about these witches with purple skin and webbed feet and melty eyes. They fly all over the world on Halloween looking for small children to kidnap and roast slowly over a fire.

But every year they all say that I'm the host, so I have to let the others tell their stories first. (Who made up that rule? I bet it was an adult.)

But at least I get to write them all down. Because I'm the best at that part. I am the Absolute Pinnacle, the Bee's Knees, the Dog's Waistcoat, the Cat's Whatever...

OK, right, the story.

This is one that Nicola told. As a special treat, she said. *Nicola's Treat* is a really stupid name for a story, though. So I am calling it *A Dog's Breakfast*.

It could also be called a shaggy dog story.

There used to be a boy in our class named Glen. I sat next to him. Not by choice.

Then Glen disappeared. The only one who knew what had happened to him was a dog. A dog I am rather fond of, as it happens.

I never liked Glen. The rest of the O'Gearys were OK, but he sucked the fun out of everything.

Actually, I hated him. He had a high, screechy voice like a burglar alarm. I hated that burglar-alarm voice.

And I hated his lies and his complaints.
He never opened his mouth except to
complain or to lie.

When he walked to school, he
complained there was too much traffic.

When the teacher asked for his homework, he lied about why he hadn't done it.

When anyone in school asked for a loan of a pencil, he complained about having to give up one of his spares.

My mother told me that he used to lie to his mum too. (Not a good idea. Mothers talk to each other.)

When his mother went to say good
night to him, when he was tucked up in
bed, she would ask if he'd brushed his
teeth, and he'd lie and say that he had.
She knew he hadn't, but if she said so,
he complained about the taste of the
toothpaste.

He kept a special packet of mints under
his pillow so he could breathe minty
breath in her face.

She found them after he disappeared.

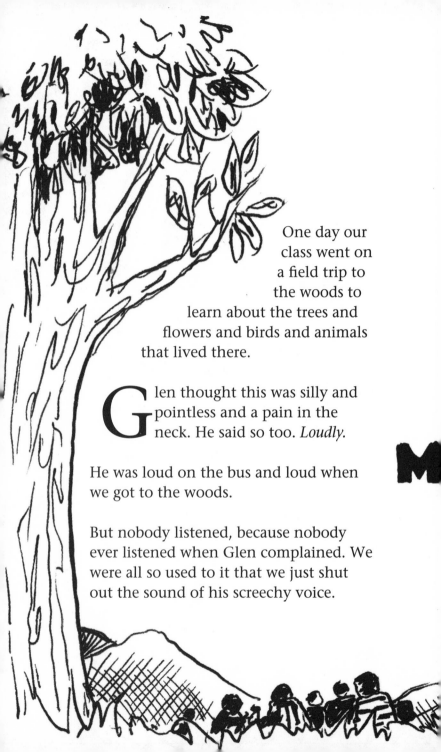

One day our class went on a field trip to the woods to learn about the trees and flowers and birds and animals that lived there.

Glen thought this was silly and pointless and a pain in the neck. He said so too. *Loudly.*

He was loud on the bus and loud when we got to the woods.

But nobody listened, because nobody ever listened when Glen complained. We were all so used to it that we just shut out the sound of his screechy voice.

That made him cross, though, and he dragged his feet while the rest of us went on ahead, hiking through the woods.

AN

MOAN

Our teacher had put us into pairs on the bus. That way, we all had someone to look out for us in case someone got lost in the woods.

And wouldn't you know it, Glen was *my* partner.

That meant I was supposed to look out for him. But I didn't.

I feel a little bit bad about that now, but if I'd hung back with him, he'd only have complained about it later.

It must have taken him a while to realize he was way behind. He was probably too busy complaining to himself that the whole idea of a woodland walk was stupid.

Anyway, he wandered off the path.
When you're in a wood you don't know,
it's very easy to get lost if you don't pay
attention. Glen wasn't good at paying
attention because he was always too busy
muttering to himself.

I can just imagine him now, looking
around, seeing nobody and snorting.
(He loved to snort.)

"Typical!" he would say. (When he
wasn't muttering to himself, he was
screeching, and in a wood on his own, I'd
say he screeched away good and loud.)
"Now I have to find my way back to the
others. And *of course* there are no signs."

That must have been when he heard the voice: "I can help you with that."

That would have made him jump,
all right! The voice had come from
nowhere, you see, or nowhere obvious,
if you get my drift. And it definitely
didn't sound like anyone Glen knew.

It wasn't anyone in his class or any of the
teachers.

That might have been a bit scary for him, I suppose. And Glen didn't like being afraid.

He'd have to turn the afraid feeling into something he liked better.

"Don't do that! Don't sneak up on me like that!" he said.

He turned
around. His eyes
were rolling in
his head, trying to
find the person with
the voice.

"Higher," said the voice, amused.

Glen looked up and saw a small person
in the branches of a tree. He couldn't tell
if the person was male or female. It was
shaped like a human, but it was small.
Not small like a child. Small like a fairy.

You're wondering how I know this, aren't you? Believe me, I have my sources.

But Glen didn't believe in fairies. "Oh, *great,*" he said. "Is this somebody's idea of a joke? It's not funny."

"I am not joking," said the person. "I can lead you back to your friends if you like. I know this forest like the back of my hand."

"It's a stupid forest," said Glen.

The person stared at him, blinking rapidly. Its eyes were more like a cat's eyes than a human's. "That's not very nice," it said. "This forest is my home, and you have insulted it."

"Don't be stupid,"
said Glen, "nobody
lives here."

"*I* live here," said the
small person.

Glen rolled his eyes.
"Yeah, right," he
said. "Up that tree, I
suppose."

"Sometimes," said the small person,
nodding. "You are not a very nice boy."

"I don't care what you say. You're not real. You're just a special effect. This is a waste of time."

Glen turned around and walked in the opposite direction from the tree the person was sitting in.

But after a few steps, there was the little person again, perched in a different tree. "You won't find them on your own, you know," the person said.

"I'm not looking for them," said Glen.
That was a lie.

"You should be," said the person.

"Why? I don't like them. They're all
boring."

The small person tilted its head to one
side. "It is easy for someone with no
imagination to be bored," it said.

"Yeah, well...you're annoying." Glen stomped past the tree the person was sitting in.

There was a *crunch* beneath his feet. At first he probably thought it was dead leaves, but it was spring and there were no dead leaves on the ground. He lifted his foot, and there was a dead snail squashed on the sole of his shoe.

"Yeurch," he muttered, scraping his shoe against a tree trunk. "Stupid snails."

A moment later, he nearly tripped on the small person, who had reappeared on the path in front of him, standing squarely on the ground with its hands on its hips.

"It's not the snail's fault that you refuse to look where you're going," it said. It was scowling now.

"If it doesn't want to get stepped on, it shouldn't live on the ground," said Glen, as if he thought that should settle it. He made as if to step over the person, but when he tried to lift his leg, he found he couldn't move.

24

"If you don't stop being such a sourpuss,
I'll do something you won't like."

"I don't like anything you do, so that
won't be hard," said Glen.

"Very well!" said the small person. It
waved its hands in the air and pointed
both its forefingers at Glen.

"The next time you set out to make another person feel bad, you'll start to turn into ... hmm ... something more useful than what you are now. If you can let a whole day pass without making anyone feel bad, you'll turn back into your old self."

It snapped its fingers and was gone.

Glen looked around, up and down the path and in the branches of the trees, but he could see nothing. He grumbled to himself and stomped down the path.

He stepped on as many snails and worms and ladybirds as he could manage.

The wood was quite small, so it didn't take him long to find the class. We were making drawings of leaves. He found me bent over a pile of young green leaves and pinched my arm.

"OW! What are you doing?"

"I got lost because of you. You're my
partner. You're supposed to watch out
for me and you didn't!"

"I'm sorry," I said, and I meant it.
"Here, I kept some paper and a pencil
for you. We have to draw three different
kinds of leaves."

Glen snatched the paper and pencil from my hand. I frowned and opened my mouth as if to speak, then stopped and sniffed the air. "Do you smell something?" I said.

"Yeah, mud and cowpats. This place is filthy."

"No, not that..." I sniffed the air again. "More like meat. It's stronger now. Did you bring a sandwich?"

"Of course I did! Everyone had to."

I glared at him, then shrugged. "Must be that, then," I said. I didn't mention that Glen's face seemed a little, well, more pink than it had been before.

Now,
here's the
thing. When
Glen went into
the bathroom to
wash his face the next morning,
he didn't recognize himself in the mirror.
I know this because I know what he was
turning into. His skin must have been
bright pink and glistening as if it was
coated with grease.

He would have been noticing the smell
too by then. The smell I'd started to
notice the day before.

Meat. Ham, to be more precise.

Very useful thing, ham, especially if you're hungry. Much more useful than Glen, though he probably didn't think that.

If he poked his cheek with his fingers,
he'd have found that his skin was damp
and soft, squidgy in a way it had never
been before.

"This is *ridiculous,*" he must have said. I can just hear him saying that. Then the look on his face when he remembered he wasn't supposed to say or do anything nasty. Not if he wanted to stop turning into something... *useful.*

But surely that didn't count. Did it? If he was the only one in the room, it couldn't possibly count. That wouldn't be fair at all!

Later that morning,
when he sat down in
his usual place at school,
I'd spread some papers over his part of the
table we shared.

I rushed to gather them up before he
started complaining, but instead of his
usual moan, he said, "Please, may I move
this stuff out of the way?"

I stared at him, my mouth wide open.
"Are you all right?" I said. "You look
feverish."

Glen wanted to say, "Don't ask stupid
questions!" I could see it in his face.

But instead, he just clenched his fists
under the table and said, "No, I'm fine.
Thank you for asking."

I blinked. "All right, then," I said and
moved the papers out of Glen's way.

The rest of the day was just like that. Every few minutes, Glen had a chance to say something mean or hurtful or rude, and every time I could see him keeping his words to himself.

It got harder and harder as the day wore on, until he could only keep his mouth shut by biting his lip and sucking in his cheeks. I watched him doing it. It was weird.

I followed him on the way home.

He went stomping down the street,
kicking the paving stones as he went. I'd
say he was imagining that each one was a
person he had been nice to that day.

"Only one day," he muttered to himself. He stared at his hands. They were as pink and soft and damp as they had been in the morning.

But no pinker, no softer, no damper. At least he hadn't gotten any worse.

He was lumbering now, as if his body felt heavy and stiff, as if his insides were glued together.

As he turned the last corner before his own street, he caught sight of a scruffy, skinny brown dog, a lanky wolfhound he had seen around before.

This, my friends, was the person—I mean, the dog—who told me the story. You may laugh, but I'm telling you, this is what happened.

43

The dog didn't belong to anyone, as
far as Glen could see. It had no collar,
and he had never seen it being walked.
Walked, ha! This wasn't that kind of dog,
for sure.

Glen came to a stop. The dog sniffed the
air and whined softly, starting to drool. It
felt hungry.

Now, Glen had bitten his lip and gritted his teeth all day instead of saying the things he was thinking. Even through the stuck-together feeling in his insides, he must have felt all of that meanness building up inside him like lava in a volcano.

He walked toward the dog. The dog barked and licked its chops. Its tongue was long and floppy, and its teeth were sharp. With a grin and a whoop, Glen stretched his leg out to kick.

Before his foot could connect, though, a voice in the air said, "Didn't think a dog would count, eh? Tsk, tsk, you are a nasty little boy."

Nobody ever saw Glen again.

And as for the dog—well, next time I saw it, it looked sleek and fat and a teensy bit smug.

And you know, a funny thing. My family has a wolfhound now. Bluebell. What a coincidence!

Dogs can't talk, you say. Huh! How else would I know all this?

THE END

Told you it was a
shaggy dog story.
That dog, it
gives me the
collywobbles. I can
still see it licking its
greasy chops.

And it is true about the
wolfhound. Nicola's family
does have one of those, all
right, but I never heard a *word* out of it.

AAAAGHHH!

Check out
all the titles in

THE

NIGHTMARE

CLUB

MIRRORED

ANNIE GRAVES

THE NIGHTMARE CLUB

GUINEA PIG KILLER

ANNIE GRAVES

THE NIGHTMARE CLUB

FRANKENKIDS

ANNIE GRAVES

THE NIGHTMARE CLUB

THE WOLFLING'S BITE

ANNIE GRAVES

THE NIGHTMARE CLUB

THE DEMON BABYSITTER

ANNIE GRAVES

THE NIGHTMARE CLUB

THE HATCHING

ANNIE GRAVES

THE NIGHTMARE CLUB